THE RISE OF
SKYWALKER

Written by Ruth Amos

Penguin
Random
House

Senior Editor Ruth Amos
Designer Sam Bartlett
Senior Pre-production Producer Jennifer Murray
Producer Louise Daly
Managing Editor Paula Regan
Managing Art Editor Jo Connor
Publisher Julie Ferris
Art Director Lisa Lanzarini

DK would like to thank Chris Gould for design assistance;
and Matt Jones and Tori Kosara for editorial assistance.

First published in Great Britain in 2020 by
Dorling Kindersley Limited
80 Strand, London WC2R 0RL
A Penguin Random House Company

10 9 8 7 6 5 4 3 2 1
001–311518–March/2020

Page design copyright © 2020 Dorling Kindersley Limited

A CIP catalogue record for this book is available from the British Library.

ISBN: 978-0-24135-775-0

Printed in China

A WORLD OF IDEAS:
SEE ALL THERE IS TO KNOW

www.dk.com
www.LEGO.com/starwars
www.starwars.com

Contents

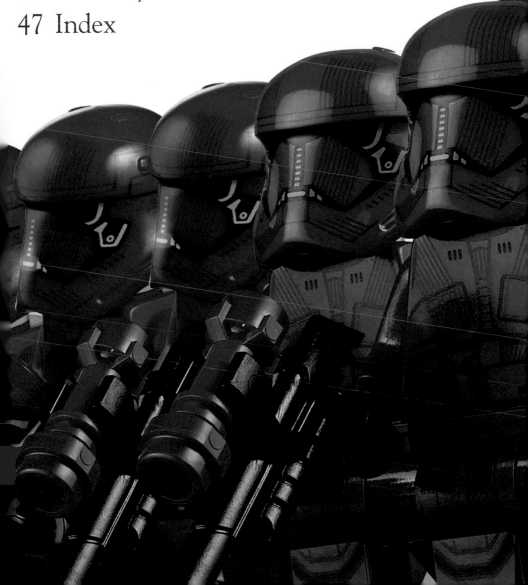

Beware the First Order

Look out! This group of villains is part of the First Order. Kylo Ren is the leader of the group. The First Order wants to rule the galaxy.

Snowtrooper

Stormtrooper

The First Order has a huge army with many soldiers. The soldiers are called stormtroopers. The army invades many different planets.

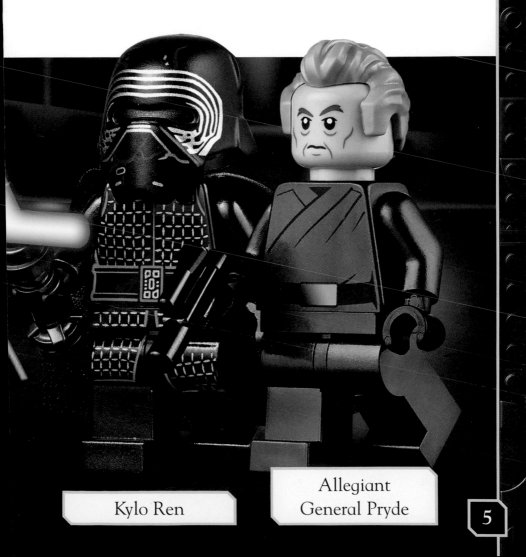

Kylo Ren

Allegiant General Pryde

Uh-oh! Supreme Leader Kylo Ren is here. He is strong with the dark side of the Force. The Force is an energy. It connects all living things.

Kylo wears a cracked helmet. He smashed his helmet into pieces when he was angry. Now it has been fixed.

Kylo leads a group of warriors called the Knights of Ren.

The Knights of Ren are fierce warriors. They follow Kylo's orders and hunt for enemies. They wear special armour and masks.

Ushar

Weapons: Thermal detonators and a big club
Equipment: Breathing tubes
Personality: Mean
Likes: Loud explosions

Ap'lek

Weapon: Ancient vibro-axe
Equipment: Smoke dispenser
Personality: Sneaky
Likes: Setting up traps to capture his targets

Kylo Ren's command shuttle swoops through space. The shuttle contains special technology. It can scan for enemies and defend itself from attacks. It has four laser cannons and two batlike wings.

The Sith are an ancient group of warriors. They use the dark side of the Force. Kylo Ren discovers a secret army of red Sith troopers.

Sith troopers do not use the Force, but they are still dangerous. They want to help Kylo Ren.

Chewbacca

Poe Dameron

Meet the Resistance

Not everybody obeys the First Order.
A small Resistance group fights
back! These heroes fight many
battles against the First Order.

General Leia
Organa

Finn

General Leia Organa is the leader
of the Resistance. The brave group
must make clever plans to defeat
the First Order.

The Resistance has set up a base on Ajan Kloss. This is a very hot and humid planet.

Ajan Kloss is covered in thick jungles. It is a great place for the Resistance to hide its fleet of ships from the First Order.

Ajan Kloss is in the Outer Rim region of the galaxy.

Major Snap Wexley is a pilot in the Resistance. Snap flies an X-wing starfighter. He uses it to go on secret spy missions.

Lieutenant Kaydel Connix is a Resistance officer. She keeps things at the base running smoothly. Kaydel is a skilled fighter.

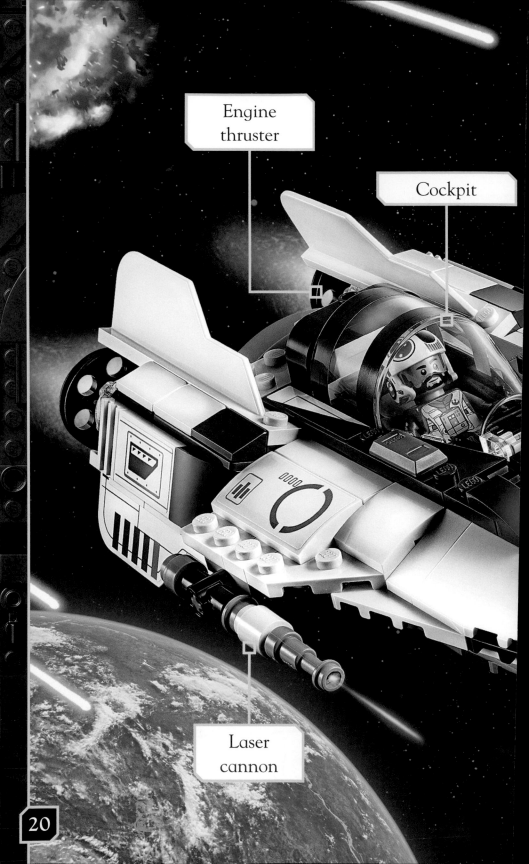

Engine
thruster

Cockpit

Laser
cannon

The Resistance has a small number of starships. This is an A-wing starfighter. A-wings are very fast and they have two laser cannons.

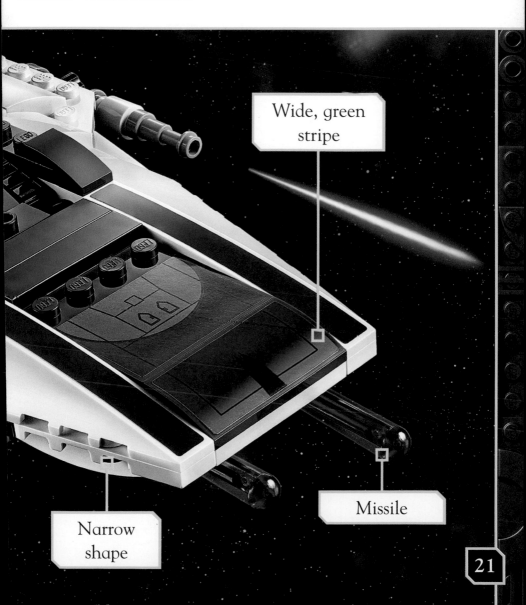

Wide, green stripe

Narrow shape

Missile

Rey is an important member of the Resistance. She is a powerful Jedi. The Jedi use the light side of the Force. Rey reads ancient Jedi books to learn more about the Force.

Rey is strong in battle. She fights foes with her blue lightsaber.

Rey duels a First Order jet trooper.

Finn believes that the Resistance can beat the First Order. Finn hopes that he and his friends can bring peace back to the galaxy.

Finn practises his piloting skills. He is also learning binary. This is the language of droids.

Chewbacca gives Finn a piloting lesson.

BB-8 is a clever, friendly droid. He rolls along on the ground. BB-8 keeps Rey company as she continues her Jedi training.

Poe Dameron is a fantastic pilot. He goes on adventures across the galaxy to help the Resistance.

Poe spots a big group of snowtroopers.

The droids C-3PO and R2-D2 work for the Resistance. Golden C-3PO speaks many languages. R2-D2 helps Poe to fly on missions.

This hairy Wookiee is Chewbacca.
His nickname is Chewie. Chewie is
a fantastic engineer. He carries a
bowcaster weapon to defend himself.

The *Millennium Falcon* is a famous starship. What are Chewie and Finn doing on the ship today?

Chewie takes a nap. Finn hides in a secret storage compartment.

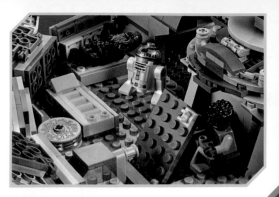

Finn helps fix a broken ship part. Chewie cooks breakfast.

Finn and Chewie play a game of dejarik.

Secret mission

Poe, Chewie, Finn and R2-D2 must find an alien called Boolio. Boolio has information about the First Order's plans.

Boolio is an Ovissian with four yellow horns. He has a secret First Order datafile. The datafile has information that might change the fate of the galaxy!

The Resistance must find the Sith world of Exegol. No one knows where it is! Rey and her friends look for clues on the planet Pasaana.

Oh no! The First Order is here! Rey and BB-8 fly off in a skimmer. A pilot chases them in a treadspeeder. Jet troopers soar after the heroes.

Who is this droid with a green nose? It is D-O! BB-8 finds him during the mission. D-O is a bit nervous, but BB-8 takes care of him.

Meet Lando Calrissian! He wears a long cape. Lando is an old friend of General Leia and Chewie. He is hiding from the First Order.

The heroes travel to the snowy planet of Kijimi. It is a dangerous world with lots of crime.

The pirate Zorii Bliss lives here. Zorii is the leader of a famous criminal gang. She wears a big, bronze helmet. Zorii does not like the First Order.

Zorii gets into her Y-wing starfighter.

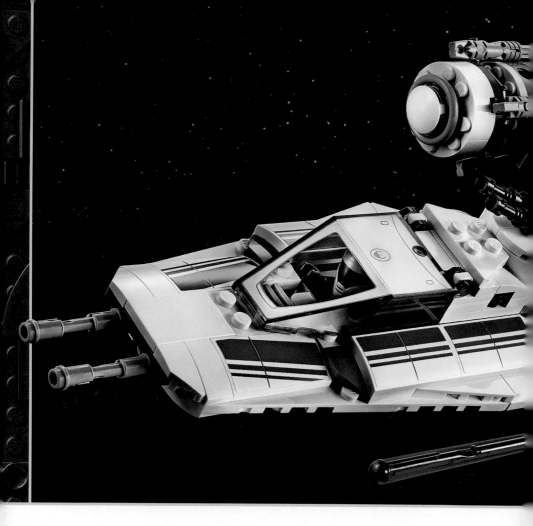

Zorii flies a Y-wing starfighter with red stripes. The Y-wing has two cannons at the front and two cannons on the top. The ship can also fire missiles.

What is next for the Resistance heroes? Rey, Poe, Chewie, C-3PO, Finn, BB-8 and D-O must continue their mission to find Exegol.

Rey must fight Kylo Ren.
The Resistance must try to defeat
the First Order and the Sith
troopers. Can they do it?

Quiz

1. Who is the leader of the Resistance?

2. Which vehicle has special technology to scan for enemies?

3. Who is Lando Calrissian hiding from?

4. What planet is the Resistance base on?

5. Who reads ancient books to learn more about the Force?

6. How many cannons does Zorii's Y-wing starfighter have?

7. What colour is the Sith troopers' armour?

8. True or false? Kylo Ren's broken helmet cannot be fixed.

9. What game do Chewie and Finn play?

10. How does the Knight of Ren warrior Ap'lek capture his enemies?

Answers on page 47.

Glossary

Allegiant General
A high-ranking officer in the First Order.

datafile
A computer file that stores information.

dejarik
A game similar to chess, which uses holograms.

droids
Another name for robots.

engineer
Someone who designs, builds and fixes machines.

fleet
A group of vehicles that work together.

humid
When the air is full of moisture and it feels damp.

Jedi
A person who uses the Force to do good.

thermal detonators
Weapons that cause explosions.

Index

Answers to the quiz on pages 44 and 45:
1. General Leia Organa 2. Kylo's command shuttle 3. The First Order
4. Ajan Kloss 5. Rey 6. Four 7. Red 8. False – Kylo's helmet has
been fixed. 9. Dejarik 10. Ap'lek sets traps for his foes.

A LEVEL FOR EVERY READER

This book is a part of an exciting four-level reading series to support children in developing the habit of reading widely for both pleasure and information. Each book is designed to develop a child's reading skills, fluency, grammar awareness and comprehension in order to build confidence and enjoyment when reading.

Ready for a Level 2 (Beginning to Read) book

A child should:

- be able to recognise a bank of common words quickly and be able to blend sounds together to make some words.
- be familiar with using beginner letter sounds and context clues to figure out unfamiliar words.
- sometimes correct his/her reading if it doesn't look right or make sense
- be aware of the need for a slight pause at commas and a longer one at full stops.

A valuable and shared reading experience

For many children, reading requires much effort, but adult participation can make reading both fun and easier. Here are a few tips on how to use this book with a young reader:

Check out the contents together:

- read about the book on the back cover and talk about the contents page to help heighten interest and expectation.
- discuss new or difficult words.
- chat about labels, annotations and pictures.

Support the reader:

- tell the child the title and help them predict what the book will be about.
- give the book to the young reader to turn the pages.
- where necessary, encourage longer words to be broken into syllables, sound out each one and then flow the syllables together; ask him/her to reread the sentence to check the meaning.
- encourage the reader to vary her/his voice as she/he reads; demonstrate how to do this if helpful.

Talk at the end of each page:

- ask questions about the text and the meaning of some of the words used – this helps develop comprehension skills.
- read the quiz at the end of the book and encourage the reader to answer the questions, if necessary, by turning back to the relevant pages to find the answers.